For L and G
"Fly high"
– H.F.

First published by Parragon in 2013

Parragon Inc.
440 Park Avenue South, 13th Floor
New York, NY 10016
www.parragon.com

Written by Margaret Wise Brown
Illustrated by Henry Fisher

Edited by Laura Baker
Designed by Ailsa Cullen
Production by Rob Simenton

ISBN 978-1-4748-6271-4
Printed in China

Away
in my Airplane

PaRRagon

Bath · New York · Cologne · Melbourne · Delhi
Hong Kong · Shenzhen · Singapore

Riding along in my

airplane, and
we will have
some fun

Over the clouds

and through the rain.

Riding along in my airplane,

Sometimes I meet a bird way up high in the sky,

Flying almost as fast as I fly—

But not as high!

into the rain

Then out of the clouds

and sun again,

Riding along in my airplane!

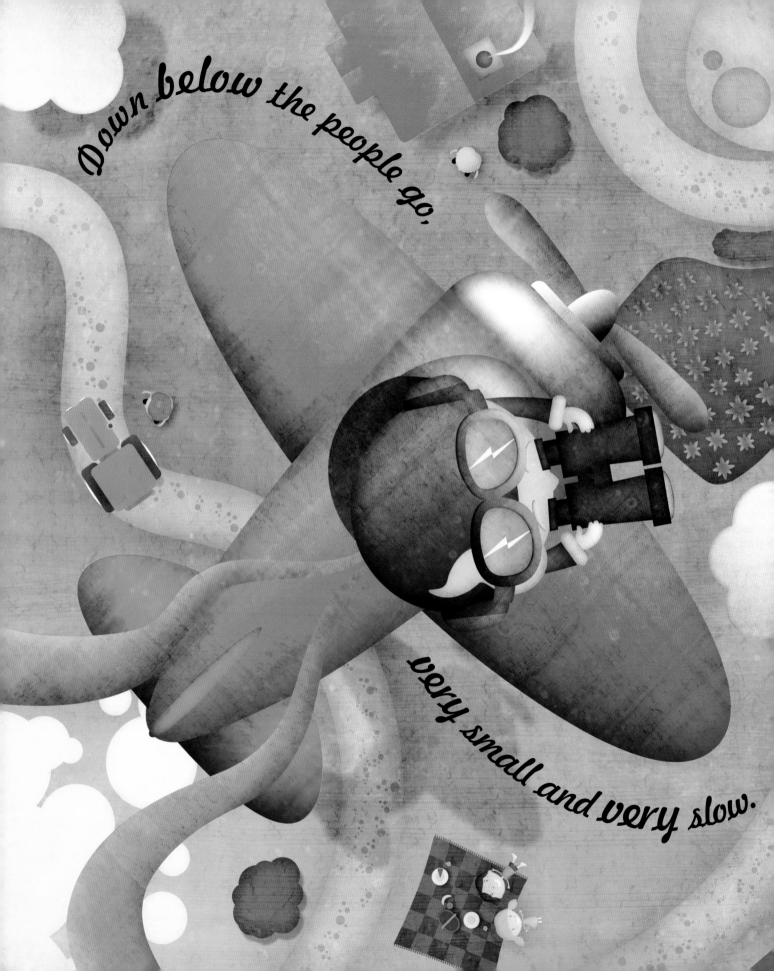

Down below the people go,

very small and very slow.

They look like bugs and ants and flies—
I wonder if they realize
What they look like to my eyes.

Riding along in my airplane,

I plunge through the sunlight,

I hurl through the rain,

Then I glide

down to the earth

in my airplane.